HOT TUB HOTEL

A T-GIRL SEXCAPADE

SHAE'S T-GIRL ADVENTURES
BOOK 2

VICTORIA RUSH

VOLUME 2

SHAE'S T-GIRL ADVENTURES - BOOK 2

COPYRIGHT

Hot Tub Hotel © 2024 Victoria Rush

Cover Design © 2024 PhotoMaras

For the uninhibited...

1
____

After my exciting affair with the hot bachelor, Aiden, I welcomed a brief respite away from his clingy embrace. As much as I enjoyed the sex with him and his spoiling me with his toys, I wasn't ready to settle down with one partner. I enjoyed my freedom and my professional life as a cabaret singer, and it had been far too long since I'd performed with my troupe. Besides, I missed the touch of a woman against my skin, and I was becoming far too dependent on Aiden's cock to satisfy my sexual needs. When Ginger invited our group to play at an upscale resort hotel in the backwoods of New England, I jumped at the chance.

It felt great to reconnect with my bandmates again and to experience the thrill of performing onstage. But after seven straight nights of singing and dancing, I was ready for a break, and after changing out of my costume, I headed toward the hotel spa for some downtime. I figured few hotel guests would be in the pool this late at night, and after putting on my bikini, I walked out into the moonlit atrium, peering at the giant empty pool. I was so focused on the lure of the glimmering, turquoise water that I barely noticed somebody lounging in the nearby jacuzzi hot tub. With her blond hair tied up in a pretty knot, she rested her head against the edge of the tub while her eyes traced the movement of my body toward the pool.

I'd intentionally worn the skimpiest swimsuit I could find to feel the therapeutic water against my skin, and as she stared at me crossing the pool deck, I could feel my nipples hardening while my bullets dented the front of my bikini, and I angled my hips away from her so she wouldn't notice the bulge between my legs from my swelling cock. But as I began to immerse myself in the shallow end of the pool, I paused just above the waterline to give her one last glimpse of my tight ass.

I was proud of my figure, and I worked damn hard to keep it firm and toned. Between my twice-weekly yoga sessions, regular workouts at the gym, and my vigorous stage routines, there was hardly an ounce of fat on my body. Even though I had a fully functional man's penis, I still looked like a young coed, with firm, natural breasts, curvy hips, a narrow waist, and an ass you could bounce a penny on. As I felt the girl in the tub eyeing me up, I smiled while I lowered my body under the surface, relieved to hide my bulging cock which was straining to burst free from my thong.

It took a while to remove the image of her sexy body lounging in the bubbly water from my mind, but as I swam across the length of the pool in the opposite direction, I felt the tension in my muscles slowly begin to ease. By the time I swam back to the other end of the pool, my cock had almost returned to its normal flaccid state, concealed neatly between the folds of my pussy in my tight bikini bottom. But when I stole another glance in her direction before flipping around, I noticed that she was still staring at me. And this time, her arms, which had previously been resting on the top of the tub, were now submerged under the surface of water as she smiled at me with an alluring grin.

Fuck! I thought to myself, feeling my cock twitching in the bottom half of my bikini. *So much for a late-night relaxing swim. I'm never going to be able to get out of this pool with my hard-on straining against my suit, as long as she stays in that tub.*

In an effort to distract myself from thoughts of what she might be doing under the foaming surface of the tub, I closed my eyes as I glided through the water using a gentle breast stroke, rehearsing the lyrics for some new songs my troupe had recently added to our playlist.

Do you wanna dance and hold my hand? I hummed Bette Midler's intoxicating song, Do You Wanna Dance With Me.

We could dance under the moonlight,
Hug and kiss all through the night,
Oh, baby, baby,
Tell me, do you wanna dance with me...

"Shit!" I spouted into the water, unable to get the picture of the pretty girl out of my mind. "That's not helping at all!"

I switched to a more upbeat tune, singing Bruno Mars' ditty, Uptown Funk,

Girls, hit your hallelujah, woo, girls hit your hallelujah,
'Cause uptown funk gonna give it to you,
Uptown funk gonna give it to you,
Saturday night we in the spot, don't believe me, just watch,
come on...

"Yes," I smiled, wriggling my hips to the groove of the song while I kicked my legs in rhythm to the beat. "That's what I'm talking about. Nothing like a good Bruno Mars song to take your mind off the distractions of the world."

By the time I'd finished swimming twenty laps replaying the lyrics for the remainder of our playlist, I'd purged the thought of the pretty girl lounging in the hot tub, and when I climbed out of the water, I glanced briefly in her direction. She was still immersed in the bubbling water with her arms concealed from view, rocking her body slowly under the waves. Whether she was simply rolling with the eddy of the current or doing something more active, I couldn't be sure. But one thing was certain as I toweled myself dry and my erection stiffened against the fabric of my bikini bottom. I wasn't going to remove the image of this sexy vixen from my mind anytime soon, and I'd either have to take matters into my own hands in the privacy of my hotel room, or join her in the tub to relieve the strain of my swelling hard-on under the surface of the water.

Fuck it, I thought to myself as I walked toward her with my towel dangling in front of my body to conceal my bulging crotch.

"Do you mind if I join you?" I said when I reached the edge of the tub.

"Absolutely," the girl smiled. "It's only the two of us here. It looks like you need to take a load off your feet almost as much as I do."

"Thanks," I said, throwing my towel to the side and slipping under the surface, thankful to hide my throbbing hard-on under the foamy water while I pulled my thong to one side, freeing my aching member.

2

"First time at Foxwoods?" the girl said, smiling up at me from the other side of the bubbling tub.

"Yes," I said, feeling my erection flapping up against my belly.

"How long are you staying?"

"A couple of weeks," I said. "I'm performing in a cabaret show at the resort."

The girl pulled her head forward and squinted at me, then nodded her head.

"I think I recognize you," she said. "Are you part of that group called the Chili Girls?"

"Yes," I chuckled. "That's us."

"You don't *look* like the other members of the group," the girl said. "Aren't they mostly female impersonators?"

"Yes," I nodded. "They're only *dressed up* as women."

"Well, you sure don't need to dress up to look like a woman," the girl said, glancing down at my plump breasts floating on top of the water. "You're *all* female, as far as I can see."

"Thank you," I said, not wanting to reveal any more details.

"So why are you part of a female *impersonator* act?"

"I dunno," I shrugged. "Maybe I just like to vamp it up on stage..."

"It's a good show," the girl said. "But you're definitely the standout. I've been keeping an eye on you for quite some time."

"I noticed," I chuckled, squirming my hips as the powerful underwater jets gushed against the top of my bobbing cock. "You're very beautiful also."

"Thank you," she said, noticing my face flushing as my erect cock swung freely from side to side. "This jacuzzi is heavenly, isn't it?"

"Yes," I said. "This is exactly what I needed for my tired muscles."

"If you position your hips in the right place," she smiled, shifting her body over a few inches. "You can direct the water jets exactly where you need it most."

"Oh, I'm feeling it in just the right spot," I grinned. "I couldn't move if I *wanted* to."

"I like how they positioned the nozzles at various places on the sides of the tub and under the bench," she nodded. "It feels even *better* if you take off all your clothes under the water."

She reached her arms around the back of her neck and untied the top half of her bikini, throwing it playfully to the side of the tub. Then she lowered her hands under the water and shimmied her body, lifting the bottom half of her swimsuit above the surface and throwing it next to the other half.

"Don't mind if I do," I smiled, following her lead and throwing both parts of my swimsuit onto the deck next to hers. "It's just us girls here."

"Mmm," she purred, writhing her hips slowly under the water. "Much better."

"Yes," I panted. "This feels even better than the pool."

"Because of the *jets*, or because you're naked?"

"Because of the *company*," I smiled, staring down at her bobbing breasts floating on top of the water. "I saw you watching me earlier. It's more fun ogling each other close up."

"What's your name?" the girl said, parting her mouth as the stimulation of the underwater jets began to have the intended effect.

"Shae," I said. "What's yours?"

"Roxanne," the girl said, suddenly catching her breath. "But you can call me *Rox*."

"That's funny," I said. "That's the name of one of my bandmates. At least her *stage* name..."

"You mean the one with a *penis*?" Roxanne said.

"I suppose so," I chuckled.

"Well, I assure you that I don't have a penis," she grinned.

"That's good to know," I grunted, positioning the spray directly at my pussy. "Because I've had my *fill* of cocks for a while."

"Oh?" the girl said, beginning to rock her body rhythmically under the bubbling water. "Do you prefer the company of *women*?"

"Sometimes," I said. "It depends on the circumstances, and the woman in question."

"Well, I'm enjoying *these* circumstances," the girl moaned, moving her arms together under the swirling water as it became obvious she was touching herself to augment the action of the pulsating jets. "And the woman in question."

"Same here," I panted, wrapping both of my hands

around my swelling hard-on and pumping it up and down while the water jet gushed over my throbbing opening.

"You're beautiful," the girl grunted, rocking her body harder under the rolling waves.

"So are you," I groaned, trying to keep myself from cumming under the water, lest I soil it for the next user.

"What are you doing under the surface right now?" Rox said as her pink nipples poked in and out of the bubbling water while she bobbed her body up and down.

"Touching myself while I direct the spray toward my pussy," I smiled, abandoning any last vestige of modesty as the two of us became increasingly candid about our desires for one another. "And trying not to cum..."

"Why not?" Roxanne said. "Let it go. I'm almost there too. I want to watch you come with me."

"I shouldn't–" I said, squeezing the tip of my throbbing organ to forestall my impending orgasm.

"Come for me, Shae," Roxanne grunted, watching a deep flush roll over the top of my chest. "I can see that you want it. Fuck, you're hot..."

"Nnngh, ssssst," I panted, feeling the floodgates starting to open as my climax took hold of me.

"Oh God, I'm cumming, Shae," Roxanne groaned. "You look so beautiful when you come."

"Oh no..." I gasped, feeling my dick suddenly pulsing in my hands while my pussy began snapping open and shut against the force of the powerful underwater spray. *"Nnngah!"*

"Yesssss," Roxanne hissed, tensing her arms in front of her body as she rammed her fingers into her hole while the two of us watched each other moaning and thrashing underwater.

Neither one of us was in a hurry to finish it, and we held our arms tightly against our shaking bodies while we smiled at each other knowingly, nodding our heads in acknowledgement of our shared pleasure.

3

———

"Shit, that was hot," Roxanne said, stretching one of her legs toward me under the water to feel the lubrication between my legs.

"Rox, wait–" I said, trying to warn her.

She sat up abruptly when her foot felt my firm erection, shaking her head at me quizzically.

"You're a man *also*?" she said, wrinkling her forehead.

"No," I said, sighing at the prospect of having to explain myself once again to another lover. "I'm what they'd call an *intersex* woman. I have all the regular parts of a woman, I just happened to have been born with a penis also."

"Lucky you," Roxanne smiled. "Talk about having penis envy..."

"You're not *turned off* by it?" I said. "Some people think trans men and women are freaks–"

"Not at all," Roxanne said. "But you're not technically *trans*. You didn't have a choice in the matter, since you were *born* this way."

"Yes," I nodded. "Thank you for being more understanding than most other people."

"We've come a long way since we used to burn people at the stake for lesser offenses," Roxanne chuckled. "Honestly, I've never thought about it, one way or the other."

"You've never thought about what it would be like to be with a trans or intersex person?" I said.

"Not until *now*," Rox chuckled.

"Does it intrigue you?" I said, probing to see if she wanted to take this any further.

"Strangely, yes," she said. "Maybe it's because you're so sexy and beautiful and look just like a woman..."

"Well, I *am* technically ninety percent female–"

"Can I *see* it?" Roxanne said. "I mean the part that's not female..."

"Right *here*?" I said, swiveling my head to make sure we were still alone in the pool room.

"Why not?" Roxanne said. "There's no one else here except the two of us, and it's after midnight, so I'm pretty sure no one else is going to come down here this late at night."

"Um, okay," I stammered. "How exactly do you want me to show you?"

"Just stand up for a moment so I can see all of you," Rox said.

"I should warn you, I'm still pretty hard–"

"All the better," Roxanne grinned. "I wouldn't want it any other way."

I straightened my legs under the water and slowly raised myself up until my bobbing hard-on poked above the surface of the water, reaching all the way up to my navel.

"Oh my God," Roxanne gasped when she saw my erection. "It's magnificent. I haven't seen a cock that big and pretty on anybody, man or women, even in my wildest dreams."

"Well, I assure you that it's not a *dream*," I smiled, tilting my hips upward to proudly display the full length of my swelling organ.

"I can see that," Roxanne said, licking her lips sensuously. "Can I touch it?"

"I suppose so," I chuckled at the usual reaction of my sex partners when they first saw me fully unclothed. Whether they were just happy to realize a long-repressed fantasy, or they were simply intrigued to see if my cock was *real*, I was always happy to oblige.

I walked slowly over the bottom of the hot tub with my hard-on waving from side to side, then I stopped a few inches in front of Roxanne's heaving chest. She stared down at my erection for a few moments, then she reached out her hands, stroking my shaft softly with the tips of her fingers.

"Does that feel good?" she said, peering up at my flushed face.

"Of course," I smiled back at her, glancing down at her pointed berries poking out of the top of the bubbling water.

"Stand a little higher," she said. "On the ledge where my feet are. I want to see your pretty cock at *eye level*."

"Okay," I said as a dribble of cum dripped out of the top of my crown, betraying my arousal from her touch. "I'm sorry that I came in the water earlier. I know that's kind of rude–"

"Normally, I'd agree," Roxanne nodded, grasping my thick shaft with both hands. "But in this case, I find it kind of *hot*."

"If you keep touching me like that, I'm going to make *another* mess," I moaned.

"Maybe we can keep it a little more contained this time," she grinned as she lowered her head over my swelling cock, circling her lips around my glans.

"Oh Rox," I groaned, watching her face bobbing over my organ. "That feels incredible..."

"Mmm," Roxanne purred as she slid one hand down to the base of my cock, slipping two fingers into my dripping slit.

While she expertly massaged my prostate gland with her flexed fingers, she simultaneously stroked my shaft with her other hand and circled her tongue around my frenulum. The combination of sensations was unreal, and it didn't take long for me to feel the familiar pangs of another orgasm rapidly building inside my hips.

"Rox, I'm going to come if you keep doing that," I panted as I held her head softly while she pumped her face over my flapping organ.

"Mm-hmm," she nodded silently, squeezing my shaft harder while she curled her fingers faster inside my swelling tunnel.

When I felt my cum rising up my shaft, I threw my head back and bit my lip trying to suppress my screams of pleasure as she held my pulsating shaft and clamping pussy while I shot one huge load of cum after another down her throat with powerful contractions. The sensation of the swirling water splashing against my hips and my ass only added to the pleasure of the experience, and I held my hips tightly against her face until the last of my honey dripped out the top of my throbbing cock.

'Holy fuck," Roxanne smiled when I finally finished coming. "That was the hottest thing I've ever done with a man or a woman. I'm sure happy our paths crossed the way they did this evening, because that was the craziest sex I've ever experienced."

"Well, it seems that we've got the rest of the night all to ourselves," I smiled, glancing around the chamber to make sure we were still alone. "And I'm pretty sure there's still room to elevate the experience, at least for *one* of us. How would you like to experience some ladyboy cock in *another* part of your anatomy?"

"Yes, please," Roxanne grinned, smiling up at me while she rubbed my leaking organ against the sides of her cheeks. "Because these water jets just aren't going to do the job any longer now that I've got a *goddess* in my presence."

4

———

"**A**re you sure you can do it again so quickly?" Roxanne said, glancing at my bouncing hard-on. "Don't you need a little more time to recover? I mean, you've already come twice–"

"Normally," I nodded, not wanting to elaborate on my unusual sexual response cycle. "But there's something about you that I find irresistible. I'm ready to go whenever you are."

"Oh, I'm *ready*, alright," Rox grinned. "I've pretty much been ready from the moment I saw you walk into the pool room..."

"Even though you didn't know I was a *ladyboy*?"

"I just knew you were *hot* and that I wanted a piece of that ass. You sure teased me long enough, swimming those long lengths of the pool while you winked at me on every turn."

"That wasn't the *only* thing winking at you," I grinned. "It took me that long to get my dick under control before I dared come out of the water."

"Well, I better get you while you're still *hard* then," Rox said, sliding my tool between her breasts and pushing them together while she flicked the tip with her tongue.

"That wasn't exactly what I had in mind," I smiled. "Though I'd love to cum all over those pretty tits. I was thinking of something a little warmer and tighter..."

"You want to *fuck* me?" Rox said. "I thought you'd never ask."

I placed my hands under Rox's armpits and hiked her up in the air, and she wrapped her legs around the back of my ass while I lowered her steaming pussy over my pole. When I was all the way inside her, I lowered our bodies slowly into the bubbling water, turning around to rest my back against the side of the enclosure while she squatted over me on the bench near one of the jets.

"Mmm," she purred, moaning softly into my mouth as I began to thrust my cock inside her. "This feels too good to be true. I've never experienced a hot tub quite like *this* before."

"Me neither," I groaned, feeling our breasts sliding together while we swirled our tongues in each other's mouths. "The feeling of the water jets spraying against my pussy while I fuck you is sublime."

"And the feeling of it squirting against my *rosebud* is equally divine. Let's make this last as long as we can."

"Okay," I smiled, slowing down my thrusting to keep myself from slipping over the edge. "Your body feels so perfect next to mine."

"And yet you have both sets of functioning sex organs," Roxanne said, taking a moment to explore my history while we paused our action. "Do you like to do it with *men* also?"

"Sometimes," I said. "It's fun to put my special features to good use with all manner of sexual partners. But there's something about a pretty woman riding my cock that I find especially enjoyable."

Rox suddenly tensed her leg muscles to stop my movement altogether.

"Wait," she said, panting heavily. "I don't want to come yet. This feels way too good."

"Uhnnn," I nodded, feeling my cock twitching in pre-orgasm while I teetered on the edge of climax. "I could stay in here *all night* doing this with you."

"Me too," Rox shuddered, squeezing her pussy against my throbbing cock. "I'm already regretting the thought of you go back to your hotel room alone. I wouldn't mind waking up this way in each other's arms."

"I like that idea," I nodded, holding her softly in the bobbing water. "How much longer were you planning on staying at the resort?"

"A couple more days," she said. "But you might be able to persuade me to stay a little longer..."

"I'm here for another week," I smiled. "You can stay with me as long as you like. Plus, I can get you a front-row seat to one of my performances..."

"I'm kind of enjoying *this* front-row seat right now," Rox grunted, beginning to rock her hips once again against my flapping erection.

"Yes," I groaned, grinding my pussy against hers while I angled my cock deeper inside her hole. "We definitely have the best seat in the house."

"Oh my God," Roxanne hissed, pressing her body harder against me. "Fuck me, Shae. I've never had sex like this with another woman before."

"So you *have* been with another woman before?" I grinned, pausing my thrusting again while I peered into her eyes. "That might be kind of fun, with *three* of us together."

"I can barely manage one and a *half*," she chuckled. "You're more than enough woman for me. Now hurry up and fuck me, I want to come on that big thumper of yours."

"Are you sure?" I said, flexing my leg muscles to keep her from sliding all the way down my pole. "Because a minute ago, you said you wanted to make this last–"

"Fuck that," Rox grunted, spreading her legs further apart to get more leverage. "I need to feel you coming inside me again. And this time, I'll be the one creaming all over *you*."

"I like the sound of that," I smiled, loosening my grip on her hips and thrusting my cock deeper inside her.

As we ground our hips together, feeling the pulse of the underwater jets gushing against our joined vulvas, we moaned into each other's mouths while rolling our tongues together in ecstasy. When I felt her utter a deep growl in my mouth and squeeze her legs tightly around the back of my ass while shaking her body against our mashing tits, I made one final thrust inside her, feeling each of us contracting together while we held each other in simultaneous climax.

"God, yes," I panted as I slowly felt her relaxing her grip around my hips. "You're exactly what I needed to ease my tension. I don't want you to leave, Rox. I want you all to myself."

"You might have to wait a bit longer," Roxanne said, turning her head in the direction of the women's change room when she heard a door on the other side of the pool suddenly swing open. "Because it looks like we're about to have some company..."

5

———

ox and I quickly separated and pushed ourselves apart a few inches while we tried not to stare at the pretty girl heading in our direction. She was a little younger than the two of us, maybe somewhere in her mid-twenties, and wearing a one-piece swimsuit that highlighted every curve of her hourglass-shaped figure. With large breasts, a narrow waist, and a beautiful curvy ass, she reminded me of the actress Salma Hayek.

"Have you got room for one more?" the girl said when she reached the side of our hut tub.

"Sure," Rox and I nodded in unison, undressing her with our eyes.

The girl glanced at the pile of bikinis lying on the deck next to us and grinned.

"You don't mind if I keep my suit on?" she said.

"Of course not," Roxanne said. "Nobody can see anything under the foamy water anyhow."

"Mmm," the girl said, slinking into the water on the opposite side of the tub and squirming her hips when she felt the powerful jets pulsating against her skin. "Now I'm beginning to understand why you took your clothes off."

"Nobody's going to mind if you do," I smiled. "It's not like anybody else is watching."

"Okay," the girl said, pulling off her shoulder straps. "I prefer bathing in the nude, anyway."

Rox and I stared at her oversize breasts bobbing on top of the water, and we reached over to touch one another while we watched the bubbling water swirling around the girl's pointy nipples.

"It feels even better if you take it *all* off," Roxanne said, squeezing my hardening shaft as I caressed her pink nub. "It's the only way to fully enjoy the sensation of the under-water jets."

The girl paused for a moment watching our arms moving under the surface of the water, then she raised her hips and pulled off the rest of her suit, flipping it onto the pool deck behind her.

"So I can see," she said, closing her eyes as she angled her hips in the direction of the closest nozzle.

"Better?" Rox smiled.

"Much," the girl sighed.

"What brings you down here so late at night?" I said, slipping my finger into Rox's slit while she began bobbing her hand up and down my erection.

"I couldn't sleep," the girl said. "I figured I might as well get my money's worth at this expensive resort while I had nothing better to do."

"You don't have a *partner* to keep you amused?" Rox asked.

"Yes, but he seems more interested in gambling in the casino and checking out the girls on the sun deck than giving me proper attention. We came here to inject a little adventure into our dull marriage, but all he seems to want to do is sleep all night long."

"You're far too young for your marriage to be getting stale so soon," I said, flexing my dick when I heard she was looking for something to spice up her sex life.

"I guess so," the girl said. "He's been hinting at trying a threesome, but I'm not ready to go that far. You know what happens when you bring a third person into the mix, it only adds extra jealousy and higher expectations."

"I suppose that depends on what *kind* of person you bring to the mix," I smiled. "Was he thinking of adding a man or a woman?"

"A woman, to be sure," the girl said. " But I don't think I could watch him having sex with another female."

"What if it were a *man*?" I said while Roxanne squeezed my dick teasingly.

"That could be interesting," she nodded. "At least he might learn one or two new techniques to please me."

"Maybe if you found one with *both* sets of parts..." I grunted when Rox inserted two fingers into my quivering pussy. "That might satisfy each of your curiosities."

"You mean like a *tranny*?" the girl said, wrinkling her forehead. "That would be kind of weird—"

"You shouldn't knock it until you try it," I panted, trying to keep my rapidly building pleasure from spilling over. "You know what they say, variety is the spice of life. Maybe that's exactly what you and your husband need to inject a little extra passion into your love life."

"I never thought about that before," the girl said, shimmying her hips on the underwater bench as she enjoyed the pulsating spray pointed straight toward her pussy. "How would that work, exactly? I mean, aren't most trannies just men with fake breasts?"

"Not all of them," I smiled. "Some of them have *both* sets of functioning organs."

"A cock *and* a pussy?" the girl said, widening her eyes as she sucked in a deep breath. "Now that would be interesting."

"What would you do with a ladyboy like that if you found one?" I said, becoming increasingly attracted to her seeming innocence.

"I don't know," the girl said, spreading her legs further apart as she directed the jet at her hardening clit. "I'd have to think about that–"

"Would you prefer to play with her *male* or *female* parts?" I continued probing.

"I'm not sure. I've never been with a woman before..."

"You're missing out then," Roxanne smiled, rolling her hips in unison with mine while we jilled each other underwater. "Only a woman really knows how to please another woman."

"I wouldn't know what to do with her," the girl grunted, feeling the water jet massaging her tingling gland.

"There are so many things you can do," Roxanne purred while she curled her fingers deep inside my pussy. "Kissing, to start. A woman kisses differently than a man. More softly and more sensuously. And not only on the mouth–"

"Oh my God," the girl groaned. "I've dreamed about that many times. What does that feel like?"

"Like your wildest dream," Roxanne smiled, noticing the girl's teats growing longer and firmer atop the surface of the roiling water. "There's nothing like the feeling of coming inside another woman's mouth."

"You've certainly aroused my interest," the girl shuddered, rocking her hips faster against the pulsating jet as she edged closer to climax.

"And don't forget the *scissoring*," Roxanne continued teasing the girl. "You haven't experienced real sex until you've enjoyed the feeling of another wet pussy rubbing against yours–"

"Oh!" the girl panted as her fingers tightened against the sides of the hot tub deck while her arms began to shake. "I want to feel that. I want to feel another woman's skin against mine. I haven't been this aroused in a long time..."

"Let it go, babe," Rox said, clamping her pussy down over my fingers, pressed deep in her hole. "Come with us while we enjoy the vision together. You're too young and beautiful to be trapped in an unhappy relationship."

"Are you *touching* each other under the water?" the girl gasped, yawning her mouth open in growing pleasure.

"Yes," Roxanne said. "And that's not the only thing we're doing–"

"Oh my God," the girl gasped. "I'm going to come. Oh *fuckkkkkk...*"

When I saw the girl climaxing directly in front of us, I grabbed my hard-on and began jerking it with two hands while Rox and I rammed our fingers into each other's convulsing pussies, groaning in unison as our bodies shook together under the bubbling water. I wasn't sure where this new connection would take us next, but something told me we were about to open our new friend's eyes in more ways than one...

6

———

"**S**till nervous about trying a *threesome*?" Roxanne said to the girl after the three of us came down from our mutual orgasms.

"Not nearly as much," she panted, glancing at the top of our breasts poking out of the water. "That was pretty hot."

"Since we seem to be getting to know one another a little better," Rox smiled. "Maybe we should share each other's names."

"I'm Amy," the girl said.

"Well, my name's Roxanne and this is Shae. And we think *you're* kind of hot."

"Thank you," Amy smiled. "I think you're both very beautiful. That is, at least as far as I can see above the waterline..."

"Do you want to come over here and get to know us a little *better*?" I grinned. "Because there's a lot more interesting parts to explore under the surface, I assure you."

"I don't know," Amy hesitated. "I'm kind of enjoying just *watching* the two of you right now."

Rox smiled at Amy, then shifted over a few inches to make room for her.

"You said you'd always dreamed of being with a woman," she said. "I'm not sure what we just did fully qualifies. Come sit between us. We won't bite."

"Okay," Amy said with a sheepish grin. "As long as we keep our bodies hidden under the water–"

"We wouldn't *dream* of exposing you," Rox smiled. "It's more stimulating with the water jets, anyway."

Amy floated slowly over to our side of the tub, then she sat down between Roxanne and me, squeezing her legs together as her ass slid against our skin.

"There now," Rox grinned. "That isn't so bad, is it?"

"No," Amy shuddered, crossing her arms over her breasts.

"You're shaking," Rox said, placing her arm over Amy's shoulder. "Come a little closer. It feels better when you have a woman's body next to you..."

"Yes," I nodded, pressing my thigh against Amy's and caressing it softly.

"You're gorgeous," Rox said, raising her hand to Amy's face and weaving her fingers through her hair. "Kiss me. You said you wanted to know what that felt like."

Amy turned her face hesitatingly in Rox's direction, then Rox lowered her face toward her lips, pausing inches away while they felt the gentle spray from the bubbling water misting over their faces.

"Mmmh," Amy groaned when Rox touched her pouting lips, sucking her upper lip into her mouth.

I ran my fingers up the top of Amy's left thigh, feeling her body trembling while the water jets gushed against our hips. She began to rock her hips softly, and when Roxanne slipped her tongue into her mouth, she pressed her face harder toward her, tilting her hips upward. I took this as a sign that she wanted me to lift my hands higher, and when I pressed my fingers between her thighs, she parted her legs, inviting me to go further. When I reached the top of her legs, I was surprised to find a thick bush covering her mound, and I ran my fingers softly through her muff, scratching her coarse hairs gently. She moaned into Rox's mouth, and Rox lowered her other hand down the front of Amy's chest, pinching her nipples while I slid my fingers over her slippery slit. Amy groaned even louder, and when I slipped two fingers between her lips, she pushed her hips forward, inserting them deeper into her hole.

"Nnngh," she huffed as I curled my fingers upward, massaging her G-spot while she rocked her hips gently against my hand.

"Yes, baby," I purred in her ear while she and Rox lashed their tongues together in each other's mouths. "Fuck my fingers. You're so soft and warm."

"Mmm," Amy nodded, beginning to rock her hips harder against my hand while Roxanne squeezed her tits. Even though neither of us knew what the other was doing under the swirling water, we seemed to sense our coordinated action, happy to let each other stimulate Amy in separate parts of her body.

I could feel my erection flapping against my belly while I fingered Amy, but I was so mesmerized by her response to my touch that I didn't even think about touching myself. With the current of multiple water jets gushing over our connected bodies, it was a sensual feast caressing her voluptuous figure while we felt her pleasure progressively building. When she began rocking her hips faster, I slid my thumb over her hardening nub, rubbing it in circles as she grunted in Rox's mouth. While Rox kissed her passionately, the sound of Amy's mews and squeals made it obvious she was going to climax soon. When I felt the inside of her pussy beginning to expand in preparation for a powerful orgasm, I slid the rest of my hand inside her cavity and pushed it deeper inside her, feeling my knuckles spreader her further apart.

"Oh my God," Amy huffed, pulling her face away from Rox as she stared into her eyes with irises as big as Saturn. "Fuck, fuck–*gahhhh!"*

When Rox felt Amy convulsing next to her, she pulled her closer, mashing their tits together while she bit her earlobe. We could both feel Amy twitching and shaking, and as her hips rocked against my ass, my hard-on slapped softly against her thigh. When she finally stopped cumming, I held my fingers gently in her twitching pussy, then I slowly pulled them out, rolling her lubrication over the top of my throbbing organ.

"Are you starting to get your money's worth *now*?" Roxanne smiled, kissing Amy around the edges of her mouth.

"That was a first for me in more ways than one," Amy nodded. "My first time with a woman, and my first time in a threesome."

"Was it as good as you imagined?" Rox said.

"I don't know," Amy grinned. "I still haven't touched either of *you* in the interesting places. I feel like I'm just scratching the surface..."

Roxanne smiled as she glanced over in my direction, winking at me knowingly.

"Something tells me my friend here has an itch she'd love for you to scratch," she said. "Would you care to switch places and feel some *other* parts this time?"

"I'd like to feel both of you," Amy nodded. "I've got a lot of catching up to do."

"I'm pretty sure that can be arranged," I nodded, smiling

toward Rox as the same thought immediately crossed both of our minds.

Amy slowly slid her hands down the front of Roxanne's chest, spreading her palms over each of her breasts while pausing to squeeze her nipples, then she turned around to do the same with me.

"How does it feel to have a *woman's* body next to you for a change?" I grinned as she pinched my nipples and bounced my tits up and down under the water.

"Strange and *delicious*," Amy smiled. "I feel like a kid in a candy store."

"Well there's a lot more candy a bit further *down*," I grunted, feeling my hard-on slapping up against my belly while Amy played with my tits.

I was tempted to give her an advance warning so she wouldn't have a heart attack when she felt my poker pointing up between my legs, but I figured it would be even more exciting for her to discover it first hand.

As she slid her hand down the front of my stomach, I gazed into her eyes, waiting to see her reaction when she discovered I was hiding something under the surface she wasn't expecting. When her fingers brushed against the end of my erection, she froze her hand, hardly believing what she felt.

"Is that a–?" she said, staring at me with a combination of surprise and excitement.

"Mm-hmm," I nodded.

"So you're a–"

"Mm-hmm," I smiled.

"But your breasts feel so–*real*," Amy said, wrinkling her brow.

"They *are* real," I said. "Just like the *rest* of my body parts."

Amy peered at me, dumbfounded for a moment, then her hand drifted a few inches lower as she pinched and stroked my erection with two fingers to make sure it was authentic.

"It's enormous," she said, wrapping her hand around my shaft and squeezing it gently. "Are you a man or a woman?"

"I guess I'm a little bit of *both*," I smiled. "But mostly *woman*. I was just born with a little extra equipment..."

Amy's hand continued drifting down my shaft, then she gasped when she felt the slit at the bottom of my pole.

"You don't have any *testicles!*" she said.

"No," I smiled. "Like I said, I'm mostly a woman."

She slid her palm gently over my cleft, then she slipped one finger into my hole.

"It feels just like mine," she panted.

"It *is*," I grunted, enjoying the feel of her probing fingers. "I just happen to have a full-grown *cock* in place of a clit."

"Does it feel good when I touch you here?" she said, pushing her fingers deeper inside me.

"Yes, just as it did when I touched you the same way a few minutes ago."

"Holy shit," Amy said, probing my entire perineum like I

was some kind of exhibit in a biology class. "This is insane. I didn't even know this was *possible...*"

"There are a *lot* of things that are possible when you have both sets of equipment like I do," I grinned, placing my hand overtop of her fingers embedded in my cunt and placing her other hand back on top of my cock. "Stroke my pole like you stroke your husband's and caress my pussy like you do your own. It's not as different as you might expect."

Amy peered at me with a flush in her cheeks, then she gripped my erection harder with her left hand while she slipped two fingers of her right hand into my slippery tunnel.

"Yes," I smiled toward her. "Stroke the entire length of my cock while you play with my pussy. I like the way you touch me..."

While Amy was concentrating on stimulating me, Roxanne pressed one of her hands underneath her ass perched on the edge of the underwater bench, massaging her clit.

"Yes, baby," I groaned as Amy caressed me. "Stroke my big dick while you finger my pussy. I want you to feel me come like you did."

Amy started jerking my cock faster, then she suddenly paused, staring down at my bobbing tits in the water.

"Why are you *stopping*?" I said, peering at her with a flushed face.

"I was hoping I might stimulate you a *different* way," she smiled. "I've never been with a transgender woman before. Would you mind if I *sat* on your cock while I stimulate your pussy?"

"Are you *kidding* me?" I said, smiling at her with a huge grin. "Nothing would please me more."

I glanced toward Roxanne who was peering back at me

with an equally wide grin, nodding towards me in encouragement.

"Maybe all *three* of us could get in on the action together
this time," I said. "After all, you said you wanted to touch
both of us to experience a true threesome."

"Okay," Amy said, peering over her shoulder at Roxanne
while Rox stimulated her from behind. "But how will we do
that exactly, with one cock and two pussies?"

"Well, technically," I smiled. "We have *three* pussies
between us. Why don't you sit on me facing towards
Roxanne, then she can sit over your hips while you grind
your pussies together at the same time."

"Holy *fuck*," Amy hissed. "I never dreamed we could do
such a thing in my wildest imagination–"

"You said you came to this place for a little *adventure*,"
Rox smiled. "Here's your chance to spread your wings."

"God, yes," Amy growled, standing up and twisting her
body away from me while she leaned her body forward,
lifting her ass toward my throbbing cock.

I placed the palms of my hands over her cheeks to find
her hole, then I pointed the tip of my instrument toward her
opening, slipping it softly inside her slippery sheath.

"Uhnnn," Amy grunted while I pressed my prick deeper
inside her hole.

As she lowered her buttocks over my hips, I curled my
hands around the sides of her back, squeezing her tits while
she angled her head backwards towards my face as I kissed
the sides of her neck. Rox placed her hands under Amy's
thighs, then she spread them upward and further apart,
squatting over my knees and sliding her hips forward until
Amy's and her pussies mashed together.

"Oh *fuck...*" Amy groaned, grinding her vulva against
Rox's as I started thrusting my dick deep inside her pussy.

"Do you like that?" Rox smiled as she slapped her tits against Amy's breasts while the three of us ground our hips together in unison. "Do you like feeling a cock and a pussy pounding you at the same time?"

"Yes," Amy groaned, sliding her hands around the back of Roxanne's ass and pulling her harder toward her while she rocked her hips against both of our hips.

"You're so hot," Roxanne said, peering at Amy's flushed face above the foaming water. "I want to feel you coming in my mouth."

As Rox lowered her face toward Amy's lips, she turned slightly in my direction so the three of us could kiss each other together. We swirled our tongues in and out of each other's mouths while we panted together in unison, feeling our climaxes building toward a peak.

"Oh God," Amy panted as she dug her fingernails into the sides of Rox's rocking ass. "I'm going to come so hard against both of your pussies. Fuck me, Shae. Fuck me hard–"

I didn't need any more encouragement, feeling my own orgasm coming on like a freight train, and as I wrapped my arms around both of their chests, I felt my cum shooting up the length of my cock while their pussies pressed against my own, convulsing together in harmony. It was the most incredible sensation I'd ever felt, and I closed my eyes, soaking up the feeling of having two women climaxing over my pulsing dick while the hot tub jets gushed toward our bodies in a symphony of pleasure.

Neither one of us said anything for the longest time, simply holding each other in the bobbing water while we savored the feeling of our three bodies joined together in post-orgasmic bliss. Rox and I took turns kissing Amy softly while we played with her breasts, feeling our vulvas sliding over one another as my cock throbbed inside Amy's pussy.

"That was incredible," Amy sighed after a long pause, sliding her hands up and down each of our arms.

"Have you picked up a few new techniques to take back to your husband to spice up your love life?" Roxanne grinned.

"Definitely," Amy panted. "But it's going to be difficult going back to one cock after this. You guys have spoiled me with a *cornucopia* of sexual delights tonight."

"Maybe you should invite us back to *your* room for the remainder of the night," Rox chuckled. "You said your husband always wanted a threesome..."

"Yes," Amy said. "But I also said I wasn't sure I could

handle the sight of him making love to another woman. I'm not sure I'm ready to share you guys with anyone else just yet."

"Oh?" I said, feeling my cock twitching inside her pussy when I discovered she wasn't finished with us yet. "What else did you have in mind? You've already experienced an orgasm with both of us–"

"But everything has been hidden under the water this whole time," Amy frowned. "I still haven't seen either of you completely naked yet. I don't want to go home without having experienced the full gamut of lesbian and ladyboy sex."

"We can go back to *my* room if you'd prefer," I smiled, happy to feel both of their bodies on soft sheets in the gentle light of the moon shining through the glass atrium of the pool.

"I'm afraid my husband will begin to worry about what happened to me if I don't get back soon. Maybe we could try something *outside* the tub before we separate for the night."

"What were you thinking, exactly?" I said, feeling my cock returning once again to its full tumescence.

"If you sat on the edge of the deck," Amy said, "I could see you in your full glory and touch you everywhere."

"What do you say, Rox?" I said, glancing toward Roxanne. "Have you had enough playing hide and seek for one night?"

"I'm game if you are," Roxanne grinned.

"Alright then," Amy said, lifting her hips off my pole and gently pushing Roxanne into the middle of the tub. "I'd never be able to sleep if I didn't see both of you naked at least once. This is going to be fun..."

Rox and I shifted over toward the edge of the tub, then

we placed our hands on the upper lip, pulling our bodies out of the pool and turning around to sit next to each other with our legs spread apart. Amy darted her eyes between our dripping bodies with her mouth agape, sighing from the thrill of seeing two naked women for the first time.

"My God, you're beautiful," she panted, rolling the tip of her tongue around the sides of her mouth unconsciously.

"Are you just going to *stare* at us the whole time?" Roxanne grinned as a dribble of lubrication rolled out of her slit and down the crack of her ass. "Or do you want a few more stories to bring back to your curious husband?"

"I wouldn't know where to start–" Amy said as she knelt on the underwater bench with the bubbling water swirling around her breasts.

"It doesn't matter where you start," I said while my cocked bobbed excitedly over my bare mound. "Because we're going to enjoy it, either way."

"I've never sucked a woman's *cock* before," she said.

"It's pretty much the same as sucking a *boy's* cock," I grinned. "Assuming you've done that before..."

"Yes," Amy nodded. "Just not a *lady*boy's cock."

"Try it and see if you can notice the difference," I said, angling the tip of my throbbing member closer to her face.

She leaned forward and brought her lips next to my bobbing dick, then she extended her tongue, flicking it softly against the underside of my swelling glans.

"Yes," I grunted. "That's the spot. Right under the rim of my crown, where it's most sensitive."

Amy placed her hands on the side of the tub to better support herself, then she leaned further forward, swirling her tongue around my coronal ridge.

"God, yes," I groaned. "You're a natural at this. Your husband is one lucky man."

"I don't do it as much as he'd like," Amy said. "You taste much better than him."

"It's probably just the chlorine from the hot tub," I chuckled. "Remind me to tell the front desk to clean the water after this. I've been a very bad girl depositing my semen in the pool."

"You mean you can come without balls?" Amy said, raising her head temporarily.

"Yes," I nodded. "I still have a prostate gland. I just don't have testicles to produce *sperm*."

"Mmm," Amy purred, lowering her head further down over my leaking erection. "Maybe *that's* why you taste so good."

She wrapped her lips around the top of my dick and began bobbing her head up and down the shaft, then Roxanne slid the fingers of one hand inside her own pussy while she toyed with her bulb with her other hand.

"Fuck, that's hot," Rox groaned, rocking her hips in synchronicity with me while Amy went down on my dick. "Finger her pussy at the same time. Shae likes that..."

"Mm-hmm," Amy hummed as she slipped three fingers into my hole.

"Sssssttt," I hissed at the feeling of her stimulating me in both places at the same time. "Bend your fingers forward while you caress the inside of my pussy," I said. "I've got a G-spot, just like you."

Amy curled her fingers in a come-hither action, and I tilted my hips forward to push them a little deeper.

"Yes," I grunted. "Flex your fingers over the front of my pussy while you suck my cock and stroke me with your other hand. It won't take long for me to come now. You're doing it perfectly."

Amy did as I instructed, and as she began to take more

of my length into her mouth while squeezing and pumping my shaft harder, she simultaneously tickled me inside with the tips of her fingers, driving me closer to the tipping point.

"*Fuck* yes," I huffed as I darted my eyes between Rox's fingers thrusting deep inside her pussy and Amy caressing me with every available part of her body. "I'm going to come, baby. You can pull off if you want. Because I'm going to spray a big load–"

"Mmmm," Amy moaned as she nodded her head excitedly, gripping my cock even harder.

When I finally exploded inside her mouth, I thought I was going to blow her face clean off my dick while I clamped my pussy tightly over her fingers, watching stars appearing before my eyes from the intense pleasure I felt emanating from every part of my body. For her part, Amy seemed to be enjoying the experience almost as much as I was, shaking her body next to mine as she angled her body forward, flapping her legs in and out while she held both of her hands tightly against her squirting pussy.

The three of us rested our bodies against the edge of the tub for a moment while catching our breath, then Amy raised her head off my organ, peering up at me with a big smile.

"*Holy shit*, girl," I smiled at her while running my fingers through her moist hair. "That was the best blowjob I've had in a long time. Are you sure this is your first time with a ladyboy?"

"Absolutely," she smiled. "But hopefully not the last."

"It looks like you've picked up a few extra tricks tonight," Roxanne grinned, glancing over at my dripping hard-on. "Whoever you and your husband decide to bring into your bed in the future, I'm pretty sure you'll be ready to please *everyone*."

"I hope so," Amy smiled. "I just hope he learns as quickly how to please *me*, because I feel like I've earned a graduate degree tonight."

9

"So you're *leaving* us, then?" Roxanne said to Amy. "We're sure going to miss you in this empty pool room."

"I guess so," Amy said. "I mean we tried just about everything, haven't we?"

"Actually," Rox smiled. "There was one thing you mentioned that we never got around to. The joy of being kissed by a girl down *there*–"

"Right..." Amy nodded. "It would be interesting to see if you can do *that* better than my husband also–"

"Which of us would you like to try it with?" Rox said, glancing at me with a playful wink.

Amy paused for a moment, peering at the two of us with a big grin.

"Maybe I could do it with *both* of you," she said. "If we arrange ourselves the right way, Shae could lick me while I lick your pussy at the same time."

"Um, yeah," Amy nodded. "That'll work. How do you want to do it, exactly?"

"How about if I lie down on the pool deck at the edge of

the tub while Shae kneels in front of me in the water, then you can kneel over my face on the other end?"

"Jesus, girl," Rox chuckled. "You really *are* learning to spread your wings tonight, aren't you?"

"Well, I've already earned my graduate degree," Amy smiled. "Why not go for my *doctorate*?"

"Okay, *doc*," Roxanne laughed. "Assume the position. Let's see how well you can apply some of the techniques you've learned so far."

I sank back into the bubbling water, then Amy lay down on the tiles at the edge of the tub, spreading her legs in front of my face. I smiled at how far she'd come since her first meeting with us, where she didn't even want to take off her clothes, let alone come out of the water. Roxanne crawled over toward the front of her body, then she turned around to face me, kneeling directly over Amy's flaring eyes.

"My God," Amy said, staring up at her dripping snatch. "I never realized how sexy a woman's pussy looks, close-up. You're exquisite!"

"It gets even *sexier* when you stimulate it the right way," Roxanne said. "Pinker, puffier, and juicier..."

"I can't wait," Amy said, raising her head and pressing out her tongue, trying to reach Rox's glistening folds.

"Hold on a sec," I said to Amy, watching a slow dribble leak out of her slit. "The key to going down on a woman is to do it *slowly and teasingly*. Don't do it like a man, beelining directly for the prize. A woman likes to build up her arousal before you get down to serious business."

"Okay," Amy said, lowering her head while she stared at Roxanne's vulva.

I paused for a moment, running my eyes over Amy's puckering pussy, then I moved my face a little closer, blowing softly on her perineum. Amy took in a sharp intake of breath, then she repeated the process with Roxanne.

"Yes, baby," Roxanne purred. "Your breath feels so cool on my skin. That feels heavenly."

"You don't want to go in and start sucking her pussy right away," I continued my instruction to Amy. "The trick is to drive her crazy with anticipation, so she's already at the height of her arousal when you begin to touch her. Try kissing her softly on the inside of her thighs and nibbling on her outer labia while she wiggles her hips..."

While I demonstrated how to do this with Amy's squirming hips, she tried to mimic my technique as Roxanne lowered her hips closer to her face.

"Mmm, yes," Roxanne groaned. "Tease me with your tongue. You're getting my juices flowing–"

"So I can *see*," Amy smiled, licking Rox's lubrication off her lips. "And *taste*."

"Do you like the taste?" Rox said, peering down at Amy's quivering stomach while I teased her softly.

"Yes," Amy said. "I could lick your pussy all day. This is way tastier than my husband's cum."

"Well there's a lot more where *that* came from," Roxanne panted. "The better you tease me, the harder the flow."

I nodded my head, noticing Amy's juices beginning to trickle out of her pussy in little rivulets.

"When you see her starting to drip out of her opening," I continued. "Lap up her juices with the flat of your tongue like you're licking a lollypop."

"A very *yummy* lollypop," Amy nodded, licking up Roxanne's juices like a puppy dog.

"Mmm," Rox groaned, pressing her pussy down harder on Amy's face. "Suck my pussy, Amy. I like watching your pretty face while you lick me."

"Pay attention to her movements and her verbal feed-back," I said. "You'll know when she's digging what you're doing. And if she tries to angle her clitoris toward your mouth, make her wait for it."

"Okay," Amy said, widening her eyes while she stared at Roxanne's swelling vulva. "I can see it poking out now. It looks like a cherry hanging from a tree branch."

"There'll be a time to *pluck* it," I nodded, noticing Amy's bulb becoming more prominent at the top of her folds. "But not yet. You want to build her anticipation before you begin to quench her thirst. Dart your tongue around the edges and rub your cheeks on her mound to bring her excitement to the next level."

I pressed my nose into Amy's bush and rolled my face over muff, breathing in her musky scent, then I flicked my tongue over the sides of her clit, being careful not to touch it directly.

"I like how you've shaved yourself," Amy panted as she rubbed her face on Roxanne's smooth mound. "It makes it easier to see everything and lick you in the right places."

"Yes," Roxanne moaned, tilting her head down so she could watch Amy teasing her vulva. "You might want to try that sometime with your hubby. Guys love a shaved pussy on a woman."

"Not as much as *I* do," Amy smiled, darting her tongue around the base of Rox's bare mound then sliding it up and down the inside of her dripping labia.

"*Fuck*, Amy," Roxanne grunted, mashing her pussy harder into Amy's face. "I need you to suck me. Please suck my clit–"

"Not yet," I smiled. "When you think she's ready, you can touch her gland, but very *gently* at first," I said, administering to Amy the same way I'd learned from my own female partners. "Surround her pearl with your lips for a moment and suck it softly into your mouth..."

"Okay," Amy groaned, struggling to maintain her composure stimulating Roxanne while I increased my focus on her. "That feels so good–"

"God, yes," Roxanne hissed when Amy took her bulb into her mouth. "Kiss my cherry. It's ripe for the plucking..."

"When you have her clit in your mouth," I continued. "You don't want to flick it too fast or too hard right away. You need to change up your technique to build her desire. One of my favorite techniques is drawing figure-eight patterns over her nub with your tongue."

"Unhhh," Amy groaned, rocking her hips faster against my face while I caressed her jewel with the tip of my tongue. "My husband always uses the same boring technique, flicking his tongue up and down like he's Gene Simmons."

"There'll be a time and a place for that," I chuckled. "But not yet. You want to wait until she's reached the plateau phase of her sexual response cycle before you begin to apply more consistent and rapid stimulation. For now, keep mixing up your licking and sucking action to keep building her arousal."

"I'm trying," Amy grunted as she swiveled her hips over my face and placed her hands over Roxanne's squirming ass, trying to keep her in position. "But you're not making it any easier for me by teasing me that way."

"Try using your *own* technique," I said, glancing up at Roxanne rocking her hips over Amy's face. "Alternate your sucking and flicking movements to make her clit even harder. When she starts moaning in regular rhythms, you'll know it's time to focus your technique more directly."

"Yessss," Roxanne hissed when Amy sucked her bean hard into her mouth, popping it in and out like a kid

sucking a lollypop. "That feels incredible. You might have missed your calling by marrying a *man*. Because you're very good at pleasing a woman."

"Maybe it's because you're a lot more *receptive*," Amy grinned, watching Rox bob her hips up and down while she sucked on her fruit like peaches in a barrel.

I glanced up and nodded approvingly at Amy's improving technique.

"When she presses her hips harder against your face, it's time to focus your sucking and licking more consistently," I said. "Once she's on the path toward orgasm, you don't want to stop or interrupt your technique. Now's the time to flick your tongue rhythmically over her bead, increasing the pace with the rhythm of her hips and the volume of her moans."

"I'm ready, baby," Roxanne nodded, mashing her pussy down over Amy's face while leaning forward to pinch Amy's pointed nipples. "Suck me *harder*. I want to come all over your pretty face."

"Mmmm," Amy nodded, rocking her hips in tandem with Roxanne as I began licking her clit harder and faster.

"If you *really* want to take it to the next level," I said, raising my head temporarily while I inserted two fingers into Amy's dripping hole. "You can stimulate the inside of her pussy at the same time you're licking her clit. Especially the part on the upper surface, a couple inches inside corresponding to the location of her G-spot. But be careful, if you do it properly, you might cause her to express her Skene's gland and squirt all over your face when she comes."

"Oh my God," Amy grunted. "I heard some women could do that. I've always wondered what that felt like."

"If you keep doing it like *that*," Roxanne groaned, tilting her hips forward when Amy inserted her fingers into her tunnel. "I'm going to gush all over you. I can feel it getting close..."

"Uhn–huft–muhhh," Amy panted as I curled my fingers harder against the front of her cavern, beginning to feel it tenting wider.

"You might feel her pussy expanding just before she climaxes," I said. "This means she's about to start contracting when she reaches orgasm. You don't want to change anything at this point. Keep doing exactly what you're doing and revel in her response to your touch. There's nothing like the feeling of making another woman climax from your touch, especially if you're doing it at the same time–"

"Yes, yes, yes," Amy huffed as she tightened her thighs around my head and began slowly raising her clenching buttocks off the deck of the hot tub. "I can feel it coming. Oh *Goddddd...."*

When Roxanne saw Amy's hips shaking over my face and a deep flush roll over her tits while she climaxed in my mouth, she leaned forward and wrapped her arms around Amy's quivering stomach while she grunted loudly, squirting a series of hard sprays over Amy's face while I simultaneously felt jets of fluid gushing around the sides of my own face. The picture of the two women squirting at the same time while they held each other's shaking bodies was too much for me, and I came hard under the water, feeling the pulsating jets pushing my erect dick from side to side. When the three of us finally finished coming, we collapsed onto one another's bodies, panting contentedly.

"That's another first for me," Amy grinned while holding onto Roxanne's dripping ass. "That's the first time I've ever *squirted* when I came."

"You're going to have a lot of surprises for your husband when you go back to your room," I chuckled. "Something tells me your marriage isn't going to be quite so boring from now on."

"Are you sure you don't want to invite us up to your room for some more fun and games?" Roxanne said. "At least to take your husband's attention off the other girls at the resort?"

"Oh, I'm pretty sure I'll be able to keep his attention focused where it belongs for the rest of our vacation," Amy chuckled.

"Well, if you decide to change your mind," I smiled. "You can find me performing in the cabaret revue playing every night at the hotel. My female impersonator routine goes way beyond just singing and dancing..."

*R*eady for more ladyboy chills and thrills? Read the next volume in Shae's T-Girl Adventures: Strip Club. Buy direct and save at victoriarusherotica.com. Or download from your favorite online bookstore here: retailer links.

It doesn't take much to bring out this couple's natural curiosity...

ALSO BY VICTORIA RUSH

Adult Fairytales:

The Enchanted Forest: An Erotic Fairytale

The Land of Giants: An Erotic Fairytale

The Dragon's Lair: An Erotic Fairytale

Witch's Brew: An Erotic Fairytale

The Mage's Spell: An Erotic Fairytale

The Mermaid Lagoon: An Erotic Fairytale

The Coven: An Erotic Fairytale

Rapunzel: An Erotic Fairytale

The Seven Dwarfs: An Erotic Fairytale

The Land of Mutants: An Erotic Fairytale

The Erotic Temple: A Sexy Fairytale (Coming Soon)

Erotica Themed Bundles:

Voyeur: Lesbian Erotica Bundle

Public Affairs: A Lesbian Anthology

Futa Fantasies: The Ladyboy Collection

Threesomes: The Lesbian Collection

Threesomes - Volume 2: The Lesbian Collection

First Time: A Lesbian Anthology

Hedonism: An Erotic Anthology

Switch Hitters: Bisexual Erotica

Taboo Erotica: The Lesbian Series

BDSM: The Lesbian Collection

Party Games: The Erotic Collection

Party Games 2: The Erotic Collection

All Girl 1: Lesbian Erotica Bundle

All Girl 2: Lesbian Erotica Bundle

All Girl 3: Lesbian Erotica Bundle

All Girl 4: Lesbian Erotica Bundle

Erotic Fairytale Bundles:

Clover's Fantasy Adventures: Books 1 - 5

Clover's Fantasy Adventures: Books 6 - 10

Erotic Fantasy:

Pirate's Bounty: A Time Travel Adventure

Wild West: A Time Travel Adventure

Private Riley: A Time Travel Adventure

Cleopatra's Secret: A Time Travel Adventure

Bounty Hunter 2125: A Time Travel Adventure

Ninja Assassin: A Time Travel Adventure

The 300: A Time Travel Adventure

Arabian Nights: An Erotic Fairytale (coming soon...)

Steamy Time Travel Bundles:

Riley's Time Travel Adventures: Books 1 - 5

Lesbian Erotica:

The Dinner Party: Lesbian Voyeur Erotica

The Darkroom: Bisexual Voyeur Erotica

Naked Yoga: Lesbian Transgender Erotica

Nude Cruise: Bisexual Voyeur Erotica

Rush Hour: Taboo Public Sex

The Girl Next Door: First Time Lesbian Erotic Romance

Girls' Camp: Lesbian Group Sex

Wet Dream: Ladyboy Fantasy Erotica

The Convent: Taboo Sex with a Nun

Sex Robot: A Dream Sex Machine

The Personal Trainer: Getting Pumped at the Gym

The Dominatrix: BDSM Lesbian Domination

Webcam Chat: Lesbian Online Sex

Paint Me: A Kinky Bodypainting Workshop

The Toy Party: Girls Sharing Sex Toys

The Costume Party: Strapping One On

Swedish Sauna: Lesbian Group Sex

The Therapist: Taboo Lesbian Erotica

Elevator Shaft: Bisexual Threesomes Erotica

Ladyboy: Lesbian Transgender Erotica

Peep Show: Lesbian Voyeur Erotica

The Dare: Public Sex Erotica

Maid Service: Lesbian Threesomes Erotica

The Hitchhiker: First Time Lesbian Erotica

The Housesitter: Spycam Lesbian Erotica

The Spa: Lesbian Group Orgy

Parlor Games: Blindfold Sex Party

The Exchange Student: First Time Lesbian Erotica

The Hostel: Bisexual Group Erotica

The Harem: Lesbian Erotic Romance

The Orient Express: Lesbian Voyeur Erotica

The First Lady: A Forbidden Lesbian Erotic Romance

The Slave: Lesbian BDSM Erotica

The Masseuse: Lesbian Sensuous Erotica

Too Close for Comfort: Lesbian Forbidden Erotica

Naked Twister: A Wild Party Game

Lexi: The Sex App (Lesbian Fantasy Erotica)

Call Girl: Lesbian Bisexual Threesomes Erotica

Circle Jill: Lesbian Masturbation Workshop

The Viewing Room: Masturbation Voyeur Erotica

Spin the Bottle: A Kinky Party Game

The Hair Salon: Lesbian Voyeur Erotica

Tribadism 1: Girls Only Sex Workshop

Tribadism 2: The Art of Scissoring

Tribadism 3: Threeway Hookups

The Kiss: A Game of Oral Sex

Pledge Week: Sorority Sisters

Carny Games 1: A Wild Sex Party

Carny Games 2: A Kinky Sex Party

Carny Games 3: An Erotic Sex Party

Dreamscape: An Artificial Reality Game

Glory Hole: Guess Who's On the Other Side

Joy Ride: A Late Night Erotic Bus Trip

The Blind Girl: An Erotic Romance(Coming Soon)

Lesbian Erotica Bundles:

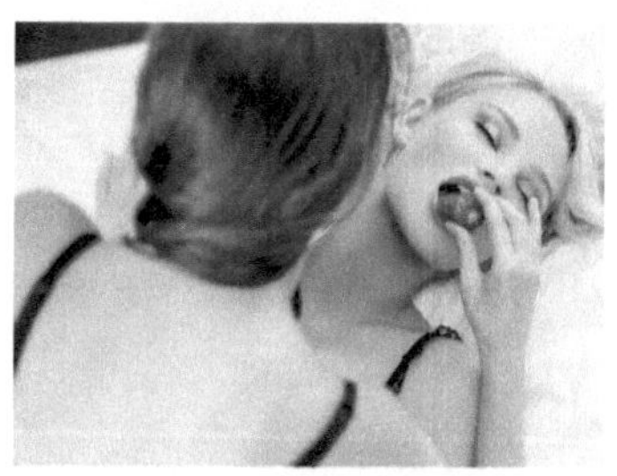

Jade's Erotic Adventures: Books 1 - 5

Jade's Erotic Adventures: Books 6 - 10

Jade's Erotic Adventures: Books 11 - 15

Jade's Erotic Adventures: Books 16 - 20

Jade's Erotic Adventures: Books 21 - 25

Jade's Erotic Adventures: Books 26 - 30

Jade's Erotic Adventures: Books 31 - 35

Jade's Erotic Adventures: Books 36 - 40

Jade's Erotic Adventures: Books 41 - 45

Jade's Erotic Adventures: Books 46 - 50

Fifty Shades of Jade: Superbundle

Standalone Stories:

The Polynesian Girl: A Lesbian EroticRomance